For Noah

First published 2005 by Walker Books Ltd, 87 Vauxhall Walk, London SE11 5HJ

10 9 8 7 6 5 4 3 2 1 © 2005 Jez Alborough The right of Jez Alborough
to be identified as author/illustrator of this work has been asserted by him
in accordance with the Copyright, Designs and Patents Act 1988 This book
has been handlettered by Jez Alborough Printed in China All rights reserved.
No part of this book may be reproduced, transmitted or stored in an information
retrieval system in any form or by any means, graphic, electronic or mechanical,
including photocopying, taping and recording, without prior written permission
from the publisher. British Library Cataloguing in Publication Data: a catalogue
record for this book is available from the British Library ISBN 1-84428-040-3

www.walkerbooks.co.uk

TALL

Jez Alborough

WALKER BOOKS
AND SUBSIDIARIES
LONDON · BOSTON · SYDNEY · AUCKLAND